This book belongs to

_____

_____

This edition published by Parragon Books Ltd in 2015

Parragon Books Ltd
Chartist House
15–17 Trim Street
Bath BA1 1HA, UK
www.parragon.com

ISBN 978-1-4723-9105-6

Printed in China

DISNEY · PIXAR MOVIE COLLECTION
A SPECIAL DISNEY STORYBOOK SERIES

FROM THE MOVIE
DISNEY · PIXAR
INSIDE OUT

PaRRagon

Bath · New York · Cologne · Melbourne · Delhi
Hong Kong · Shenzhen · Singapore · Amsterdam

At the moment a little girl called Riley was born, an Emotion named Joy stepped up to a console at Headquarters, inside Riley's head.

Joy saw Riley's parents on the screen as it flickered to life.

"Hello, Riley," said Mum.

"Oh look at you," said Dad. "Aren't you just a little bundle of joy."

Because Joy was at the console, Riley felt happy and a new happy memory was created.

In Headquarters, a golden sphere rolled across the floor towards Joy and she picked it up. It showed Riley as a baby. The sphere was gold because the memory was happy. Joy turned and placed the sphere on an empty shelf at the back of Headquarters.

Joy returned to the console. She touched it and heard Riley making happy baby noises.

Just then, Joy noticed somebody standing next to her.

"I'm Sadness," said the newcomer.

Sadness touched the console and baby Riley began to cry. Joy quickly took control again.

"Can I just ..." Joy said. "I just want to fix that. Thanks."

As Riley grew older, the shelves at Headquarters became full of memory spheres, mostly golden happy ones. From there, they made their way through vacuum tubes that led to Long Term Memory in Riley's Mind World.

Joy and Sadness were joined by three more Emotions – Fear, Anger and Disgust.

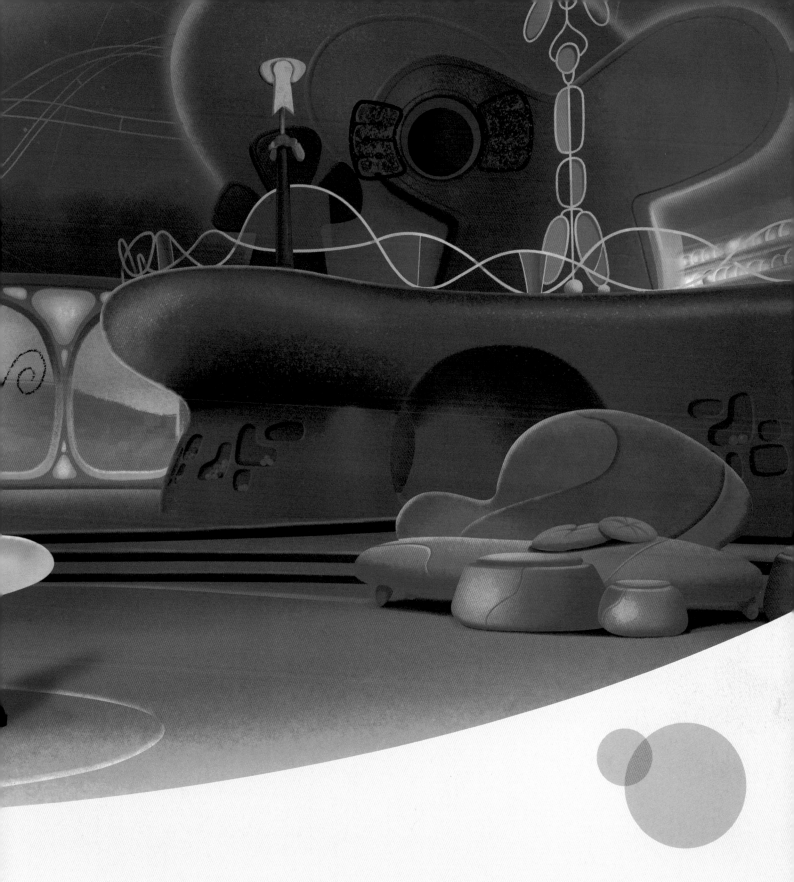

Together, the Five Emotions made important choices for Riley. But Fear, Disgust, Anger and Sadness usually wanted Joy to drive at the console. After all, they wanted Riley to be happy as often as possible.

Fear helped to keep Riley safe.
He once stopped her from tripping over
a power cable when she was playing.

Disgust kept Riley
away from things that
looked, smelled or tasted
funny. Like broccoli!

Anger cared very deeply about things being fair for Riley. Most of Riley's tantrums happened when Anger was driving the console.

Finally, there was Sadness.
Her role was not as obvious as
Riley's other Emotions. In fact,
Joy wasn't sure why Sadness was
there at all.

When something really important happened to Riley, a core memory was created. These went into the core-memory holder and powered Riley's Islands of Personality.

Riley had five islands – Family, Honesty, Hockey, Friendship, Goofball. These were the things that were most important to her. Each island was like a mini theme park in her mind. When Riley played around with Dad, Goofball Island was in full swing!

One night, just as 11-year-old Riley was ready to go to sleep, the Emotions watched as Mum and Dad tucked her into bed. As she fell asleep, the screen in Headquarters went dark.

"Woo! Another perfect day!" Joy called happily, looking at the wall of brand-new golden memories.

"Alright, we did not die today," said Fear. "I call that a success."

"We love our girl," Joy continued. "She's got great friends, a great house, things couldn't be better. After all, Riley's 11 now. What could happen?"

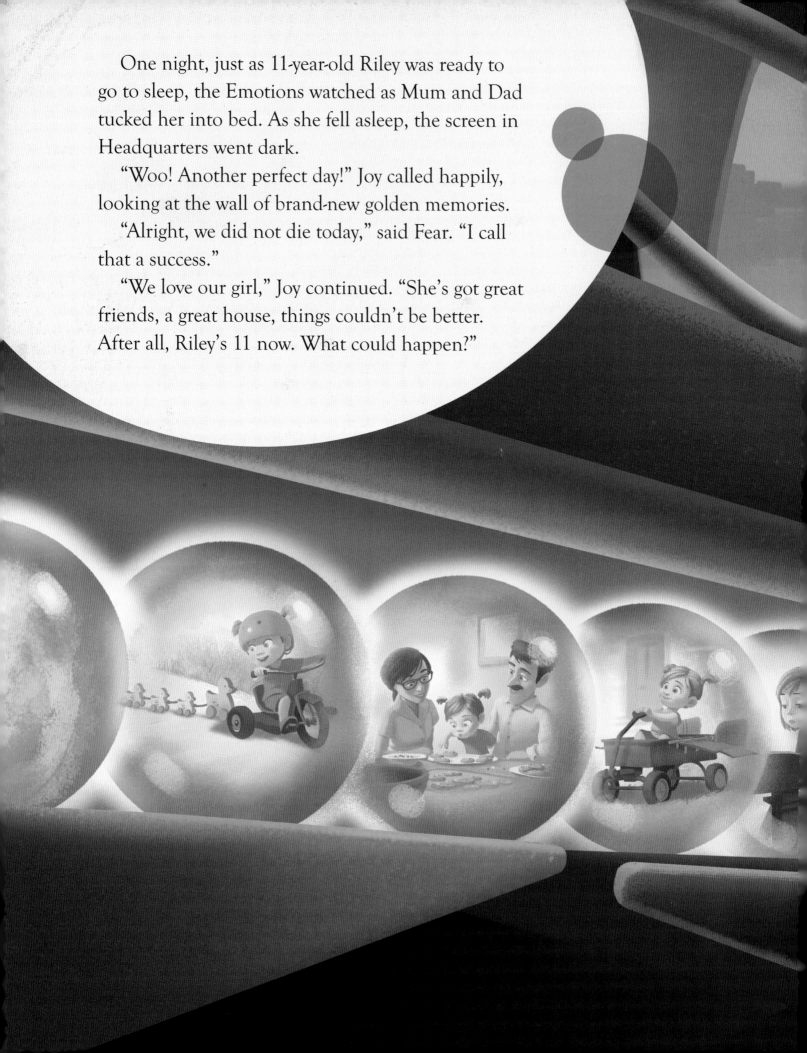

Joy soon got her answer. The very next day, Mum and Dad announced they were moving from their hometown in Minnesota to San Francisco!

On the long car journey, while the other Emotions were panicking, Joy tried to cheer everyone up.

"Hey look!" she said. "The Golden Gate Bridge! Isn't that great? It's not made out of solid gold like we thought, which is kind of a disappointment, but still!"

When the car finally stopped outside their new home, Riley's Emotions were speechless. The house looked old and dreary. To top it all off, the moving van was lost, so Riley had none of her things!

Through all of this, Joy desperately tried to keep Riley's memories happy. She took control of the console and helped Riley to look on the bright side.

Before long, it was Riley's first day at her new school.
She said goodbye to her parents and headed out of the door.
In Headquarters, Joy gave each of the Emotions an
important job to do. She carefully drew a chalk circle around
Sadness's feet.

"This is the circle of Sadness," Joy explained. "Your job
is to make sure that all the Sadness stays inside of it."

At school, the teacher asked Riley to stand up and tell the class something about herself. Smiling shyly, Riley shared a happy memory of playing hockey back in Minnesota. But suddenly, her smile faded.

In Headquarters, Joy realized that Sadness had touched the hockey memory, turning it blue!

"Sadness!" Joy scolded. "You touched a memory!"

The blue memory was now stuck, looping in Riley's mind. Back in class, she was starting to cry.

While Joy, Anger, Fear and Disgust tried to dislodge the memory, Sadness took control of the console. As Riley cried in front of her new class, her first ever blue core memory was created.

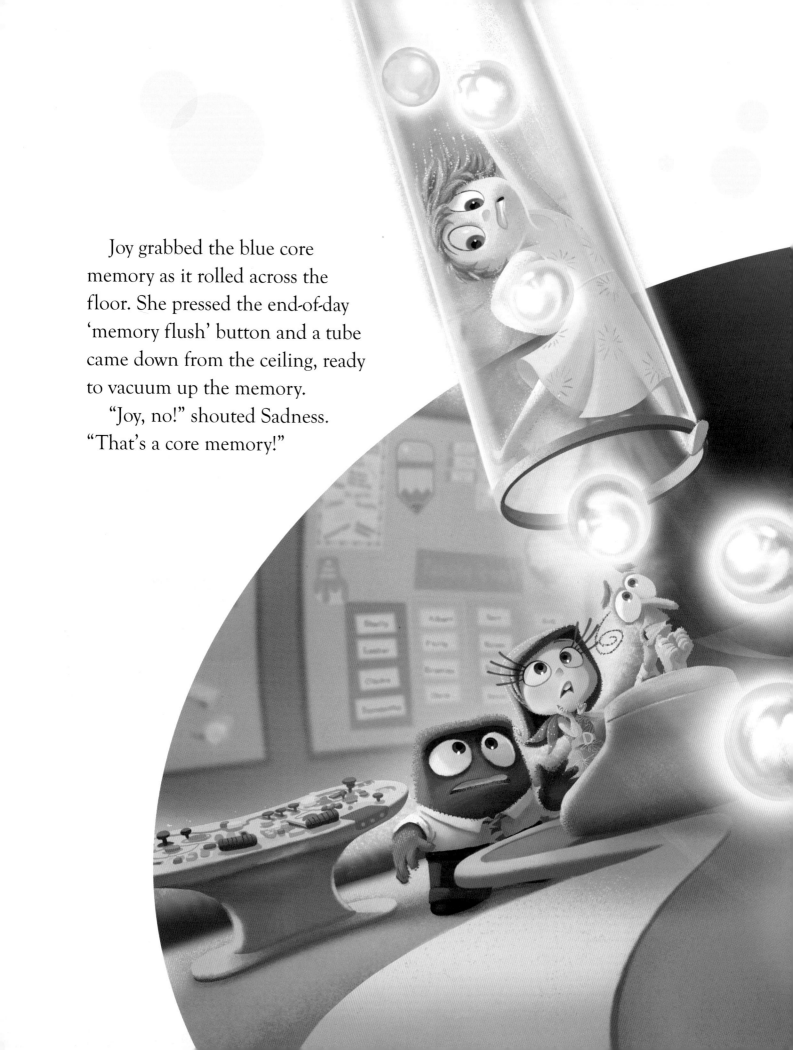

Joy grabbed the blue core memory as it rolled across the floor. She pressed the end-of-day 'memory flush' button and a tube came down from the ceiling, ready to vacuum up the memory.

"Joy, no!" shouted Sadness. "That's a core memory!"

Sadness tried to grab the blue memory back from Joy. As the two struggled, they knocked into the core-memory holder and the five golden core memories fell out! Outside the window, the Islands of Personality went dark.

"Aah!" Joy cried, scrambling to collect the memories.

In the chaos, Joy, Sadness and all six core memories got sucked into the memory flush tube!

They travelled through Riley's mind and were finally dumped out in Long Term Memory. All of the Islands of Personality were still dark. Joy knew they had to get the core memories back to Headquarters to get the islands working again!

But Headquarters was far away. The only route back was across a bridge to Goofball Island and then along a lightline – which was like a power cord – that linked the islands to Headquarters.

"But what if we fall into the Memory Dump?" asked Sadness. "We'd get forgotten forever!"

"Yeah, no, we won't fall," Joy answered. "Just think positive."

She collected up the core memories and began crossing the bridge, leaving Sadness behind.

That evening, Riley was having dinner with Mum and Dad.
They were asking Riley about her day at school.

"It was fine, I guess. I don't know...." Riley answered grumpily.

Riley's parents were shocked. They couldn't understand why
their daughter wasn't her usual, happy self.

At Headquarters, Disgust was driving the console. With Joy and Sadness gone, the remaining three Emotions were trying their best to keep Riley acting normal, but it wasn't working!

"Riley, is everything okay?" Mum asked.

"Ugggghhhh!" Riley sighed.

"Riley," said Dad. "I do not like this new attitude."

Just then, inside Riley's head, Anger took over the console. "Oh, I'll show you attitude, old man," he said.

At the dinner table, Riley lost her cool. "Just leave me alone!" she shouted at her shocked parents.

"That is it!" Dad shouted back. "Go to your room! Now!"

Riley stormed upstairs and slammed her bedroom door.

Meanwhile, Joy and Sadness were on the lightline to Headquarters when Goofball Island began to crumble behind them – it was collapsing because Riley had stopped goofing around with her dad!

The two Emotions scrambled back across the island and reached the Long Term Memory cliff just before the island fell into the pit below.

Joy tried to stay positive. They would just have to find another way back to Headquarters.

Sadness slumped to the floor.

"Just one thing," she said. "I'm still in an emotional slump and my legs aren't working yet. Just give me a few ... hours."

So Joy picked up one of Sadness's legs and dragged her into the maze of Long Term Memory shelves. Joy had to get back to Headquarters before Riley forgot Joy existed!

At that moment, Riley was chatting to her old friend, Meg, on her laptop. Meg lived back in Minnesota and had just told Riley there was a brilliant new girl on their hockey team. Riley missed playing with her old team, so hearing about a new girl made her feel angry.

At Headquarters, Anger took charge of the console.

"Hey hey," said Disgust. "We do NOT want to lose any more islands!" But Anger had already pushed a button.

"I gotta go," Riley said and slammed her laptop shut.

Over in Long Term Memory, there was a horrible groaning sound as Friendship Island fell into the dump.

"Ohhh, not Friendship!" Joy exclaimed. She looked down at the friendship core memory in her arms as its colour faded.

"Goodbye friendship, hello loneliness," said Sadness.

Desperate to get to Headquarters, Joy led Sadness back into the maze
of Long Term Memory. They soon ran into a funny-looking creature.
"You're Bing Bong!" Joy realized. "Riley's imaginary friend!"
Riley and Bing Bong used to play together – they even had a rocket

But over the years, Riley had forgotten him. Bing Bong's dream was to rocket to the moon with Riley again, so Joy suggested he come to Headquarters with them.

"Ha ha!" Bing Bong cried, dancing around happily.

Bing Bong offered Joy a bag to carry the core memories. He also had an idea – they could take the Train of Thought back to Headquarters!

"There's a station in Imagination Land," Bing Bong said. "Come on, this way!"

The trio reached Imagination Land just as the train pulled away – they'd missed it. Luckily, Bing Bong knew where another station was.

"Right this way, through Imagination Land!" he called, leading them through the huge gates.

Once inside, Joy and Sadness were amazed. There was French Fry Forest, Trophy Town and Cloud Town! Joy leaped onto a small chunk of cloud and floated into the air. "Ha ha!" she cried. "It's so soft!"

They soon reached a House of Cards. Bing Bong rushed inside
and reappeared with his rocket wagon.

"Now I'm all set to take Riley to the moon!" he called.

Suddenly, a handsome teenage boy rolled out on a conveyor belt.
A worker explained that the boy was an Imaginary Boyfriend.

"I would die for Riley," the Boyfriend said.

"Ugh!" said Joy. Then she, Bing Bong and
Sadness carried on towards the train station.

Meanwhile, Riley was at the try-outs for her new hockey team. At Headquarters, Fear had recalled every single hockey memory to fill the core-memory holder. He didn't know what else to do! He thought one of them would surely be able to replace the missing hockey core memory.

Out on the ice, Riley tried to hit the puck but missed and fell over. Fear's plan hadn't worked. Anger pushed Fear aside and took over the console. Riley threw down her hockey stick and stormed off the ice.

Inside Riley's mind, Hockey Island crumbled and sunk into the Memory Dump.

Joy, Sadness and Bing Bong had almost made it to the train station when some Mind Workers suddenly took Bing Bong's rocket wagon. They threw it into the Memory Dump!

"No!" cried Bing Bong. "Riley and I are going to the mooooon!"

He sat on the floor and started to cry sweets. Joy tried to cheer him up, but nothing worked. She could hear the train – they had to hurry!

Sadness sat beside Bing Bong. "I'm sorry they took your rocket," she said.

"It's all I had left of Riley," Bing Bong replied.
After they had talked a bit longer, he said,
"I feel okay now."

Bing Bong stood up. Joy was
surprised. Sadness hadn't made
Bing Bong feel worse, she had
made him feel better!

Joy, Sadness and Bing Bong made it on to the train, but it stopped when Riley went to sleep! They headed to Dream Productions, where Riley's dreams were created. A special filter made everything look completely real to Riley.

Suddenly, Sadness had an idea. They could create a scary dream to wake up Riley and get the Train of Thought moving again!

Joy liked the idea, but she thought it would be better to wake up Riley with happiness.

"That's never happened before," said Sadness.

But Joy was excited about her plan. She found a cute dog costume and told Sadness to put on the back half. Together, dressed as a dog, they ran onto the set of the dream, while Bing Bong looked after the bag of core memories.

Back at Headquarters, Fear was on
dream duty. He was watching the dog run
around on-screen and finding it a bit dull.
But suddenly, the dog split in half!
At Dream Productions, Sadness and Joy had
come apart in the dog costume.

Joy was now chasing Sadness around the set. Through the reality filter, it looked pretty scary!

As Riley began to stir, the Dream Production guards realized what the newcomers were up to. Joy and Sadness hid, but Bing Bong was arrested!

Bing Bong was taken down into Riley's Subconscious, which contained her deepest fears. Joy and Sadness went to rescue Bing Bong and they met a huge, scary clown called Jangles. This gave them an idea. They took Jangles back to Dream Productions and he stomped through the set. Riley woke up!

Meanwhile at Headquarters, Anger had plugged an idea bulb
into the console. After everything that had happened, and without
Joy around to help, Anger had decided the best thing for Riley to
do was run away – back to Minnesota. This idea came into Riley's
head just as she awoke from her scary dream.

At that moment, Joy and Sadness were back on the Train of Thought, which was moving again. Joy turned to Sadness.

"Hey, that was a good idea about scaring Riley awake," she said.

"Really?" said Sadness. She was glad to know she'd been helpful.

The pair found a memory sphere on the train and discovered it was one they both loved. Sadness remembered it was the day that Riley's hockey team lost the playoffs when she missed the winning shot. Joy loved it because the whole team had come to cheer Riley up.

Later, at Riley's house, Riley sneaked downstairs and secretly borrowed Mum's credit card to buy a one-way bus ticket to Minnesota!

At that moment, the tracks underneath the Train of Thought began to crumble. The train crashed and its passengers fell to the ground! Joy looked up to see a huge space where Honesty Island used to be – it was gone!

"That was our way home!" Joy cried. "We lost another island ... what is happening?"

"Haven't you heard?" replied a Mind Worker. "Riley is running away."

After the train crash, Sadness realized they could use a recall tube to get back to Headquarters. Joy and Sadness stepped into the tube, but Sadness accidentally touched a core memory and it turned blue. Sadness stepped away when she saw what she had done. Joy began travelling up the tube alone, but the cliff underneath began to break apart. The tube broke and Joy fell, deep into the Memory Dump!

"Joy!" Sadness cried.

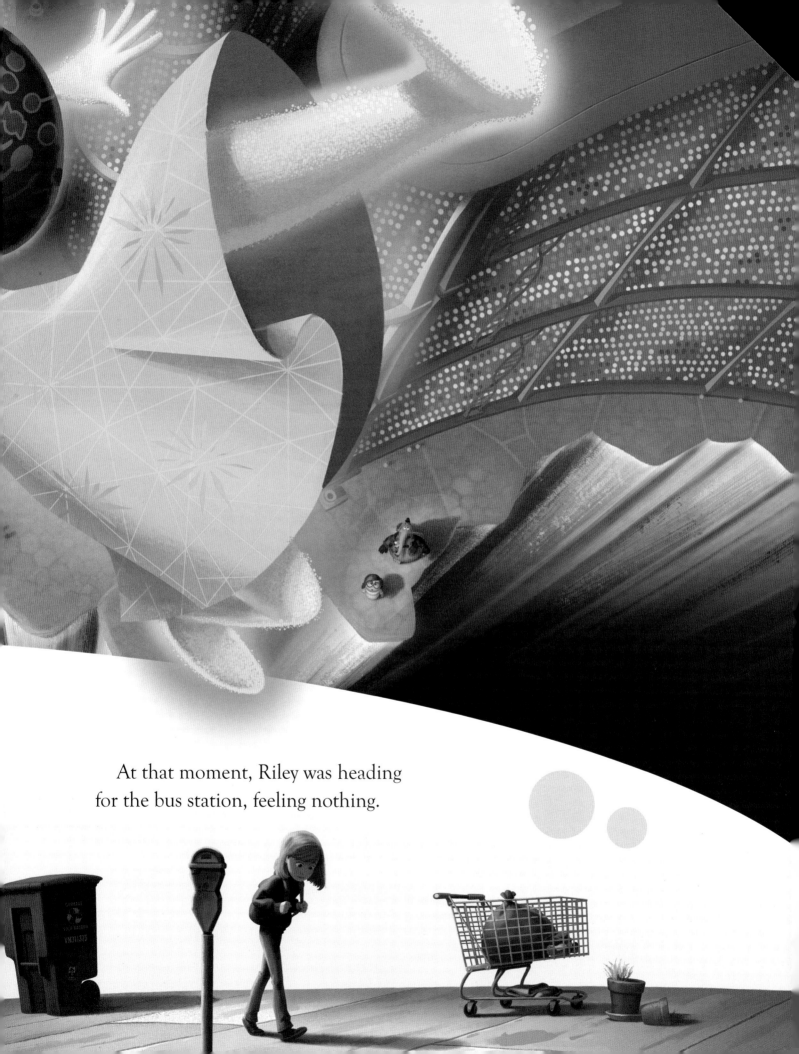

At that moment, Riley was heading
for the bus station, feeling nothing.

Down in the dump, Joy felt hopeless. She looked at the memory with the hockey team cheering for Riley.

One of Joy's tears fell onto the sphere and, as she wiped it away, the memory rewound and turned blue! Joy saw that Riley had been sitting, sad and alone, before the happy part of the memory. She suddenly realized that Sadness was important.

"The team ..." she mumbled, "they came to help because of Sadness!"

Just then, Bing Bong appeared. He and Joy came up with an idea – they could use the rocket to escape the Memory Dump!

They sung loudly to power the rocket, but each time they flew up, they couldn't reach the top of the cliff. Joy was about to give up, but Bing Bong urged her to have one more go. This time, without Joy noticing, Bing Bong jumped out of the rocket before it left the ground. Now that it was lighter, the rocket with Joy inside soared up and landed safely on the cliff.

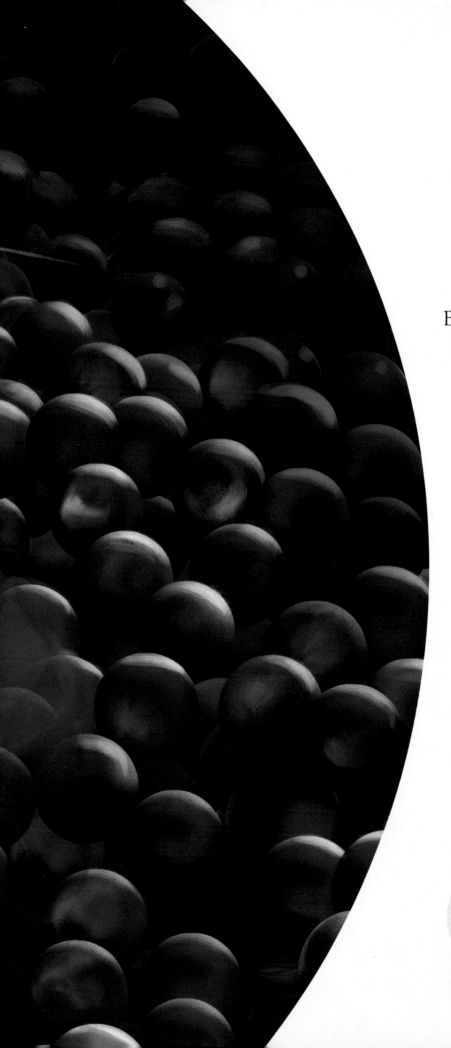

When Joy realized what
Bing Bong had done, she
looked over the edge of the
cliff and saw him far below,
dancing with happiness.
"Go save Riley!"
he called. "Take her to
the moon for me, okay?"
"I'll try, Bing Bong,"
Joy replied sadly.
"I promise."
Then Bing Bong took
a bow and disappeared.
Riley didn't need
him anymore.

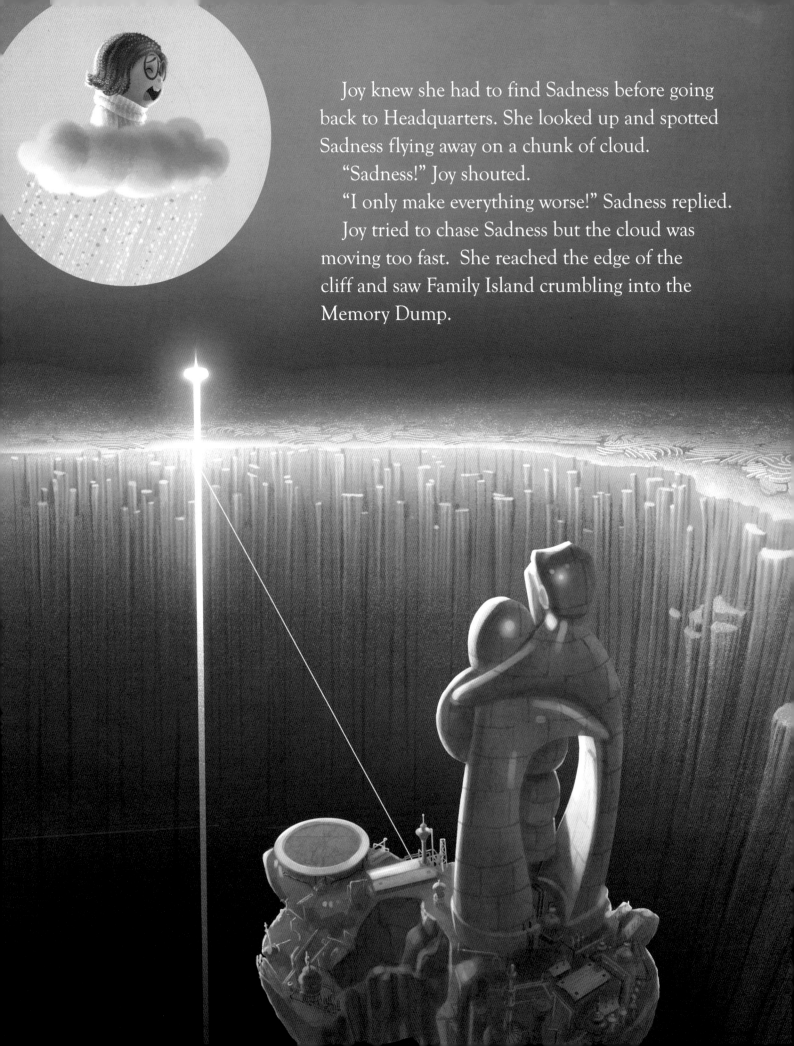

Joy knew she had to find Sadness before going back to Headquarters. She looked up and spotted Sadness flying away on a chunk of cloud.

"Sadness!" Joy shouted.

"I only make everything worse!" Sadness replied.

Joy tried to chase Sadness but the cloud was moving too fast. She reached the edge of the cliff and saw Family Island crumbling into the Memory Dump.

Then Joy spotted Riley's Imaginary Boyfriend
sitting alone nearby. She had an idea!
Joy used the Boyfriend
Generator to make hundreds
of Boyfriends. Using them
as a huge tower, she swung
towards Sadness.....

"Joy?" Sadness said.

"Gotcha!" Joy cried as she grabbed her in mid-air. "Hang on!"

The two flew through the air towards Headquarters. SPLAT! They hit the back window and slid down the glass.

Anger, Fear and Disgust ran to the window. How were they going to get Joy and Sadness inside? Disgust had an idea. She taunted Anger until he got mad and lit up in flames. Disgust picked him up and used the fire to cut a hole in the window! Joy and Sadness climbed inside.

"Oh, thank goodness you're back!" cried Fear.

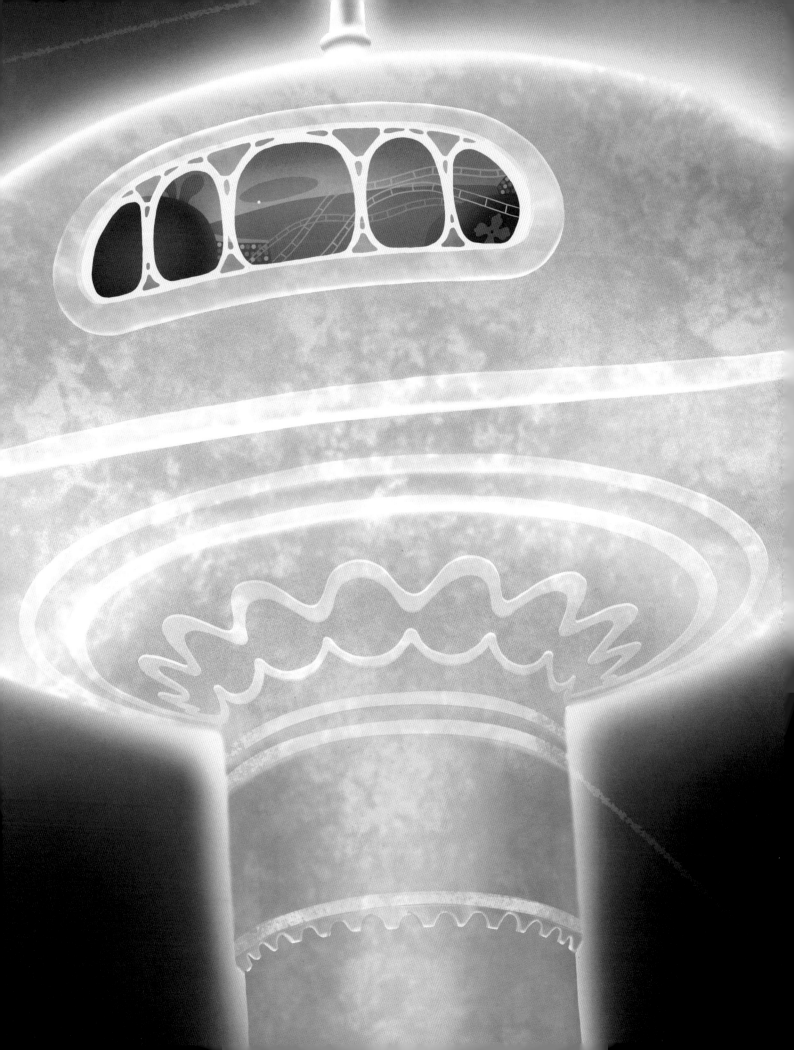

Joy looked up at the screen and saw that Riley was on the bus, ready to run away from San Francisco and her parents.

"Sadness," Joy said, "it's up to you."

"Me?" Sadness replied. "Oh ... I can't, Joy!"

"Yes you can," said Joy. "Riley needs you. Go!"

Sadness took a deep breath, stepped up to the console and pulled out the 'run away' idea bulb.

On the bus, Riley's face suddenly changed from totally blank to very sad. She stood up. "Wait!" she called out to the driver. "I want to get off!"

At Riley's house, Riley had just arrived back home. Mum and Dad had been worried sick. In Headquarters the other Emotions looked on as Joy handed the golden core memories to Sadness. The spheres all slowly turned from gold to blue! Sadness placed them in the memory projector.

As Riley's memories of her old friends and home came into her mind, she began to cry.

Riley told her parents how she felt. "I miss home," she said.
"Please don't be mad."

"We're not mad," said Dad, as he and Mum hugged Riley.

At Headquarters, a new half-blue, half-gold core memory
rolled in and generated a brand-new Family Island. A few days
later, all the Islands of Personality had reappeared, with a few
extra ones, too!

"We've been through a lot lately," said Joy. "But we still love
our girl. After all, Riley's 12 now ... what could happen?"

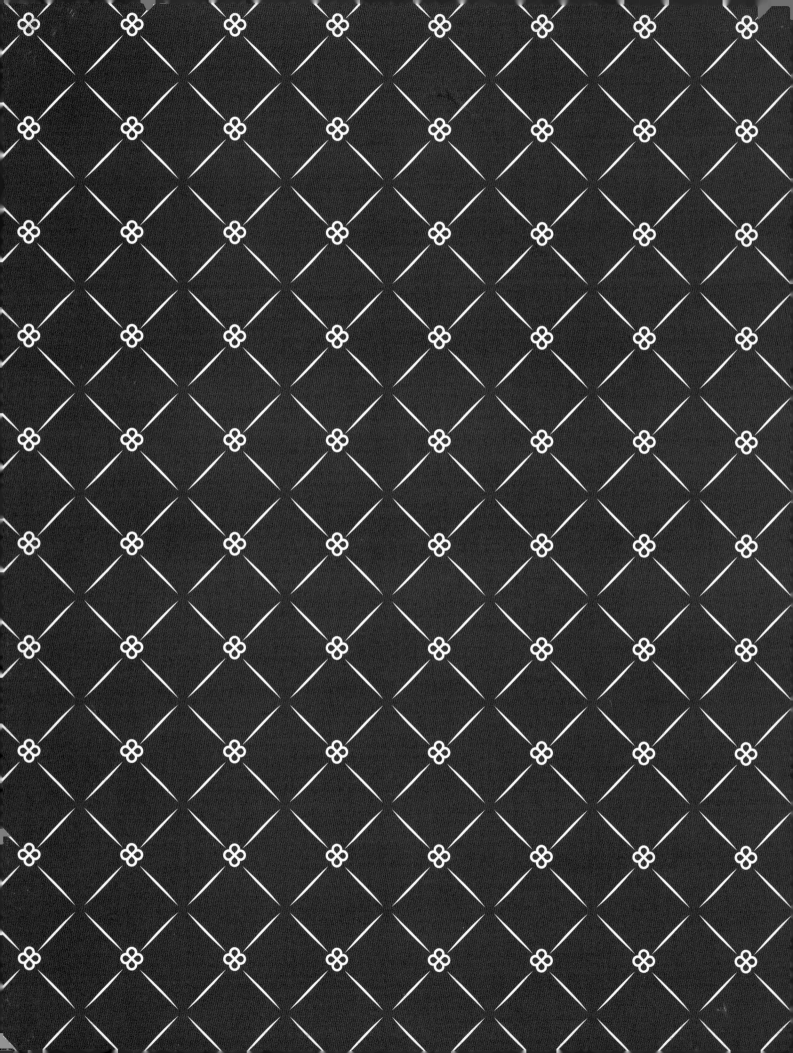